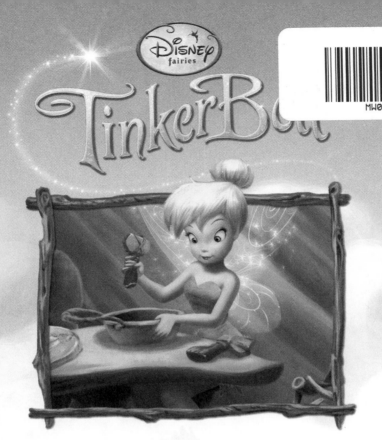

A Guide to Pixie Hollow

Adapted by Elle D. Risco
Illustrated by Studio Iboix and the Disney Storybook Artists

A Random House PICTUREBACK® Book

Random House 🏠 New York

Copyright © 2008 Disney Enterprises, Inc. All rights reserved. Published in the United States by Random House Children's Books, a division of Random House, Inc., 1745 Broadway, New York, NY 10019, and in Canada by Random House of Canada Limited, Toronto, in conjunction with Disney Enterprises, Inc. Pictureback, Random House, and the Random House colophon are registered trademarks of Random House, Inc.

Library of Congress Control Number: 2008922051
ISBN: 978-0-7364-2368-7

www.randomhouse.com/kids/disney

Printed in the United States of America
10 9 8 7 6 5 4 3 2
First Edition

Close your eyes and imagine a magical land. . . .

A land where fairies use their special talents and a bit of pixie dust to put the finishing touches on nature. Flowers are painted by hand, snowflakes are individually frozen, rainbows are spun from water and sunshine—and all four seasons exist at once!

Here live the Never fairies of Never Land. Let them take you under their wings and show you around this wonderful place called Pixie Hollow!

Never Land

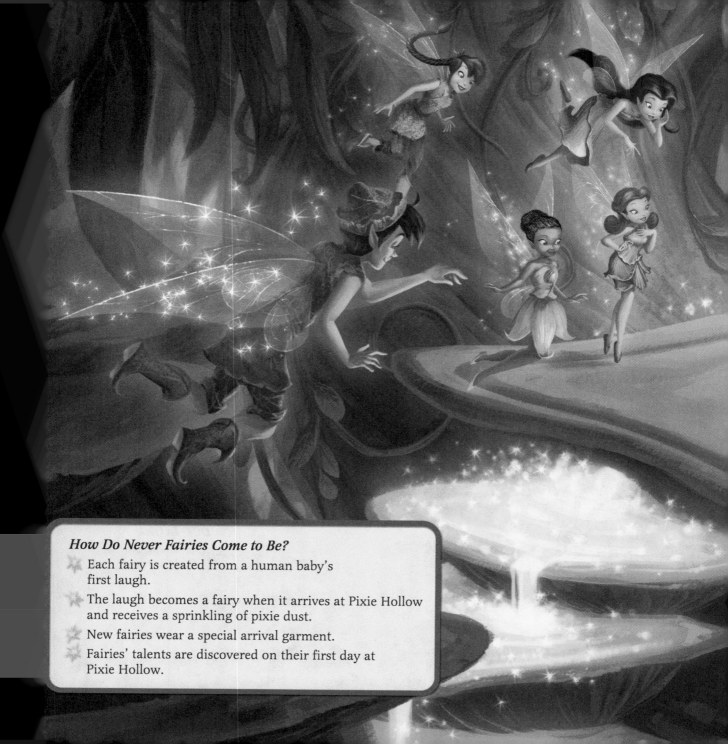

How Do Never Fairies Come to Be?

- Each fairy is created from a human baby's first laugh.
- The laugh becomes a fairy when it arrives at Pixie Hollow and receives a sprinkling of pixie dust.
- New fairies wear a special arrival garment.
- Fairies' talents are discovered on their first day at Pixie Hollow.

How does a fairy get to this tiny wonderland? It's easy! Just take flight and follow the Second Star to the Right. Ride the breeze, cross the sea . . . and before you know it, there you are!

Welcome to Tinker Bell's house! Like every fairy's home, Tink's is special in its own way. From her house, she has a great view of the tinker fairies' village.

Rosetta's House

Silvermist's House

Iridessa's House

Fawn's House

Meet Tinker Bell

❀ She's a tinker fairy who loves to invent things.

❀ She's determined, curious, and sometimes impatient.

❀ Look for her stylish leaf dress, green slippers, blond hair, and long bangs.

Lilypad Pond is the peaceful home of the water fairies. The sound of lapping streams and tiny waterfalls is relaxing and musical. While touring the pond by leaf boat, you might see water fairies collecting dewdrops from spiderwebs or sculpting water like clay!

Meet Silvermist

- "Sil" is a water fairy who can talk to babbling brooks.
- She's encouraging, sympathetic, and quick to lend a hand.
- Look for her long, dark hair and her water-lily-petal dress.

The fields and meadows of Pixie Hollow are filled with colorful flowers and plants of every type that bloom here year-round. Gentle garden fairies can revive wilted blossoms with a sprinkling of pixie dust. These fairies also take care of young bulbs, making sure they get off to the right start!

Meet Rosetta

Rosetta is as pretty as the roses in her garden.

She's nurturing, and loves color, beauty, and sweet-smelling things.

Look for her dainty rose-petal dress and shoes and her perfectly arranged red hair.

It's impossible to be anything but bright-eyed and lighthearted in Sunflower Meadow! Filled with sunflowers, this is the home of the light fairies. The sunbeams streaming through the golden petals are dazzlingly beautiful. Here, light fairies play jump rope with beams of light and gather sunlight in buckets!

Meet Iridessa

- "Dessa," a brilliant light fairy, is smart and organized.
- She creates and captures colorful rainbows!
- Look for her twinkling eyes, dark hair, and sunflower-petal skirt and shoes.

Meet Fawn
- Fawn can talk to and comfort animals.
- She's confident and energetic—a rough-and-tumble tomboy.
- Look for her long braid, orange-moss tunic, and leaf pants.

At Pine Tree Grove, you can get an up-close-and-personal look at Pixie Hollow's wildlife. Animal fairies take care of all the furry, fuzzy, and feathered creatures—and will even join in a game of leapfrog! Fairies' homes can be found right next to birds' nests and chipmunks' hideaways!

The best place to find fairies is the Pixie Dust Well, located in the Pixie Dust Tree at the heart of Pixie Hollow. At sunrise, every fairy comes here to get a daily dose of pixie dust. It's the perfect spot for fairies to catch up on gossip and talk about their plans for the day.

Meet Terence

Terence is a dust-keeper fairy.

He makes sure each fairy gets just the right dose of pixie dust—not too much, not too little.

Look for his golden hair, acorn cap, and leaf vest.

One of Tinker Bell's favorite places is the tinkers' workshop in Tinkers' Nook. This is where tinker fairies carve acorn buckets, weave baskets, and fix wagons, pots, pans, and anything else that needs repairing. Tink is almost always here working on her newest inventions.

Berry/Nut Squasher

Berry-Paint Sprayer

Most of Pixie Hollow is safe and carefree. But there are a few things to watch out for.

First, avoid Needlepoint Meadow, where the Sprinting Thistles grow. These tall, prickly weeds race around, trampling or poking anyone in their path!

Second, beware of hawks! These fierce forest hunters can whisk away a fairy in an instant!

And third, watch out for Vidia. She's the only fairy who can ruin someone's day with one mean remark.

Meet Vidia

❀ Vidia is the fastest fairy in Pixie Hollow— and she knows it.

❀ She lives by herself in a sour-plum tree.

❀ Impatient and conceited, Vidia is annoyed by everyone.

While all four seasons exist at once in Pixie Hollow, it's the Never fairies who make the seasons change on the mainland. With each new season, the fairies have much to do.

As winter comes to an end and spring approaches, the fairies prepare everything from berry paint for coloring flowers to rainbow tubes full of rainbows. In a glorious procession, they carry their creations across the sea to bring the magic of spring to the world!

Other Highlights of the Year

- In winter, snowflake and frost fairies craft tiny details in ice crystals.
- In fall, the autumn fairies paint the bright yellow, orange, and red colors on all the leaves.
- In summer, the summer fairies chase dragonflies in green meadows bursting with sunshine!

There's so much to discover and explore in Pixie Hollow. You know the way—head toward the Second Star to the Right and fly straight on till morning. When you arrive, all your fairy friends will be waiting for you!